Tips for Reading Together

Children learn best when reading is fun.

- Talk about the title and the pictures on the cover.
- Look through the pictures together so your child can see what the story is about.
- Read the story to your child, placing your finger under the words as you read.
- Have fun finding the hidden starfish.
- Read the story again and encourage your child to join in.
- Give lots of praise as your child reads with you.

Children enjoy reading stories again and again. This helps to build their confidence.

Have fun!

Find the starfish hidden in every picture.

Funny
Fish

Written by Cynthia Rider
Illustrated by Alex Brychta

OXFORD
UNIVERSITY PRESS

Mum   Dad   Biff

Chip   Kipper   Floppy

Kipper was fishing.

He got a hat.

Biff was fishing.

She got a crab.

Chip was fishing.

He got an octopus!

Mum was fishing.

She got a bucket.

Dad was fishing.

He got a boot.

SPLASH!

Floppy got a fish!

Think about the story

Why do you think Floppy fell into the water?

Who do you think caught the funniest fish?

What would you do if you caught a big crab, like Biff?

Floppy's fish lives in the sea. Where else do fish live?

Tangled lines

Follow the lines to see who gets the fish.

More books for you to enjoy

Level 1: Getting Ready	Level 2: Starting to Read	Level 3: Becoming a Reader	Level 4: Building Confidence	Level 5: Reading with Confidence
The Snowman	Poor Old Rabbit!	Missing!	Arctic Adventure	The Hairy-Scary Monster
Funny Fish	Super Dad	The Old Tree Stump	Looking After Gran	The Golden Touch
Picnic Time	The Monster Hunt	The Raft Race	Hungry Floppy	The Lost Voice
Silly Races	I Can Trick a Tiger	The Real Floppy	Shrinking Powder	The Palace Statues
Dad's Birthday	Floppy and the Bone	Dragon Danger	Husky Adventure	The Secret of the Sands
Mum's New Hat	Ouch!	The Spaceship	Trapped!	Mountain Rescue

OXFORD
UNIVERSITY PRESS

Great Clarendon Street,
Oxford OX2 6DP

Text © Cynthia Rider 2005
Illustrations © Alex Brychta 2005
Designed by Andy Wilson

First published 2005
All rights reserved

British Library Cataloguing
in Publication Data available

ISBN 978-0-19-838554-7

10 9 8 7 6 5 4

Printed in China by Imago

Have more fun with Read at Home

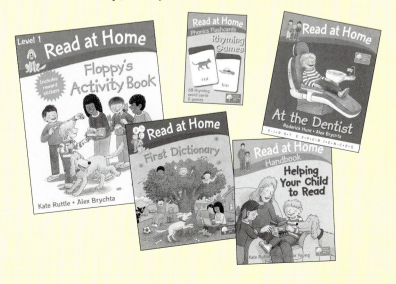